Miss Brooks' Story Nook

(where tales are told and ogres are welcome)

STORY BY

Barbara Bottner

ILLUSTRATIONS BY

Michael Emberley

ALFRED A. KNOPF *New York*

Miss Brooks has Story Nook first thing before school, and I don't like to miss it.

But whenever I take the shortcut past Billy Toomey's house,

he grabs my hat and yells, "I'm going to get you, Missy!"

It's vexing.

So mostly, I take the long way to school.

But today it was raining and I was late. . . .

I slipped into Story Nook.

Then, suddenly,

there was a crack of thunder.

All the lights went out!

"It's too dark to read. So let's huddle in close and make up our *own* tales," said Miss Brooks.

"I mainly like to *read*
stories," I said. "Not tell them."

"Good readers make
wonderful story*tellers*," said
Miss Brooks.

In a squeaky voice, Violet said,
"I *love* the dark. Maybe we'll see ghosts!"

"Violet loves ghosts more
than anything," said Plum.

"I love *stories* more than anything," said Miss Brooks.
"So let's close our eyes and let our minds wander.
Everyone has a tale to tell."

"I've got nothing," I said.

"One way to begin is to think of a problem
that needs solving," said Miss Brooks.

My problem was Billy
Toomey. But there was no
way I was going to make
up a story about *him*.

"Or sometimes," said Miss Brooks, "you can start with an interesting character."

Wilbur said aliens in spaceships were interesting.

Violet said she liked ghosts.

Plum thought aliens and ghosts were too scary.
I thought it would take more than aliens or
ghosts to scare Billy Toomey.

I wondered if *anything* would. . . .

"An ogre lives down the street from me . . . ," I said.
"*That's* interesting," said Wilbur.
"Really?" said Violet. "An ogre?"
"Yes, and she has a bunch of wild animals for pets."

"That's an excellent start!" said Miss Brooks.
"What kind of animals?"

"Graciela has a lion, an alligator, and maybe a couple hyenas. And disgusting smells drift up from her basement. Probably from the snake."

"Why doesn't she just have a dog?" Wilbur asked.

"According to Graciela, snakes make great pets. She doesn't have to walk them and they don't bark."

"I'd rather hear about kittens," said Plum.

"Ghosts," said Violet.

"Now what happens, Missy?" asked Miss Brooks.
"Stories need action."

"Graciela's snake gets out of its cage."

"But then Graciela catches it right away. The end!" said Plum.

"Not so fast!" I said.

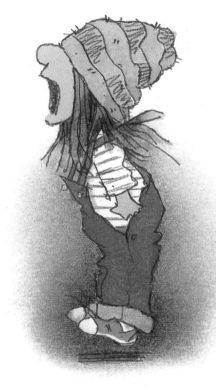

"You're right, Missy," said Miss Brooks. "This story needs more plot— what happens next?"

"Her snake slithers up the street to that exasperating Billy Toomey's house," I said.

"It wraps around him and squeezes so hard, his eyes pop out. He won't be bothering anyone anymore."

"Whoa!" said Wilbur.

"I guess that takes
care of Billy Toomey!"
said Violet.

"Why can't
there be kittens?"
whimpered Plum.

"And poor Graciela," I said, on a
roll now, "came to a wretched end."
"Really? *How* wretched?" asked
Miss Brooks.

"Well, her lion finished her off.
She's dead, dead, dead."

"Is she a ghost now?" asked Violet.
"Why would you get rid of Graciela?
She wasn't bothering anyone!" said Plum.

"Plum has a good point, Missy. We all like stories
to have satisfying endings," said Miss Brooks.
So I said, "Okay, she doesn't get eaten. . . ."

"Instead," said Wilbur, "Graciela gets on a spaceship and returns to her planet!"

"Too lame!" I said.
"The Kitten Planet?" said Plum.
"Too tame!"
"The Ghost Planet," said Violet.

"All Violet's stories are the same," said Wilbur.

"I'd like to know what happens to that snake," said Miss Brooks.

"Well," I said, "Graciela decided snakes might be too much trouble after all."

"So what did she do with it?" Plum asked.

Storytelling was full of questions.

"She gave it to me!" I said at last.

"But what will *you* do with it?" Wilbur asked.

Suddenly, the lights came back on. Story Nook was over.

But my story still needed an ending. . . .

The next morning I wasn't late, but I took the
shortcut to school anyway.

When Billy Toomey said, "I'm going to get you!" I was ready.
I gave him my best snake-eyed stare and said:

"Hey, Billy, did I ever tell you about the enormous, slimy boa constrictor my neighbor Graciela gave me?

"It hisses and flicks its tongue, and slithers around the

neighborhood, sniffing out its favorite meal . . ."

"... which is exasperating boys like YOU."

At Story Nook, Miss Brooks asked, "Did you think more about how to end your story, Missy?"

"I did. And I told the whole slimy tale to Billy Toomey."
"Really? What did Billy think?"

"He *loved* it!"

I loved it too! It was a revolting
tale with a happy ending.

And I made it up myself.

For Miranda and Brandon, Valerie amd Geoff
—B.B.

For Liz G. and Deb P., who together inspired Miss Brooks,
and for Violet, the original woolly hat Missy
—M.E.

THIS IS A BORZOI BOOK PUBLISHED BY ALFRED A. KNOPF

Text copyright © 2014 by Barbara Bottner
Jacket and interior illustrations copyright © 2014 by Bird Productions, Inc.

Visit us on the Web! randomhouse.com/kids

Educators and librarians, for a variety of teaching tools, visit us at
RHTeachersLibrarians.com

Library of Congress Cataloging-in-Publication Data
Bottner, Barbara.
Miss Brooks' Story Nook / by Barbara Bottner ; illustrated by Michael Emberley. —First edition.
p. cm.
Summary: A school librarian encourages her students to make up stories, and teaches a lesson about bullying in the process.
ISBN 978-0-449-81328-7 (trade) — ISBN 978-0-449-81329-4 (lib. bdg.) — ISBN 978-0-449-81330-0 (ebook)
[1. Storytelling—Fiction. 2. Bullies—Fiction. 3. Librarians—Fiction.] I. Emberley, Michael, illustrator. II. Title.
PZ7.B6586MI 2014 [E]—dc23 2013013799

The illustrations in this book were drawn with pencil, scanned,
then printed onto Arches 90 lb. hot press watercolor paper using waterproof inks,
then painted with tube watercolors.

MANUFACTURED IN CHINA

August 2014

10 9 8 7 6 5 4 3 2 1

First Edition